CHLOE

Peter McCarty

Balzer + Bray

An Imprint of HarperCollins*Publishers*

To Suki

Balzer + Bray is an imprint of HarperCollins Publishers.

Chloe. Copyright © 2012 by Peter McCarty

For information address HarperCollins Children's Books, a division of

HarperCollins Publishers, 10 East 53rd Street, New York, NY 10022.

www.harpercollinschildrens.com

Library of Congress Cataloging-in-Publication Data is available.

ISBN 978-0-06-114291-8 (trade bdg.) — ISBN 978-0-06-114292-5 (lib. bdg.)

Typography by Martha Rago

12 13 14 15 16 LP 10 9 8 7 6 5 4 3 2

❖

First Edition

Chloe loved the end of the day, when her whole family was together. She called it family fun time.

She had a father and a mother,

ten older brothers and sisters, and ten younger brothers and sisters.

Chloe was in the middle.

One evening Dad brought home a surprise: a new television.

"We can all watch it after dinner."

Chloe was not so sure about this idea.

Soon, everyone came to the table for peas, carrots, lettuce,

broccoli, asparagus, noodles, and sweet potatoes, all their favorite foods.

After dessert, all the Bunnies crowded around the television.

Everyone except Chloe and little Bridget.

"Chloe, you're missing it," said Billy. "Pound Cake is attacking the city!"

"Hey, get out of the way!"

"This is the worst family fun time EVER!" Chloe said.

"Bridget and I know how to have fun."

What was this?

What did Bridget find in the box?

It was bubble wrap.

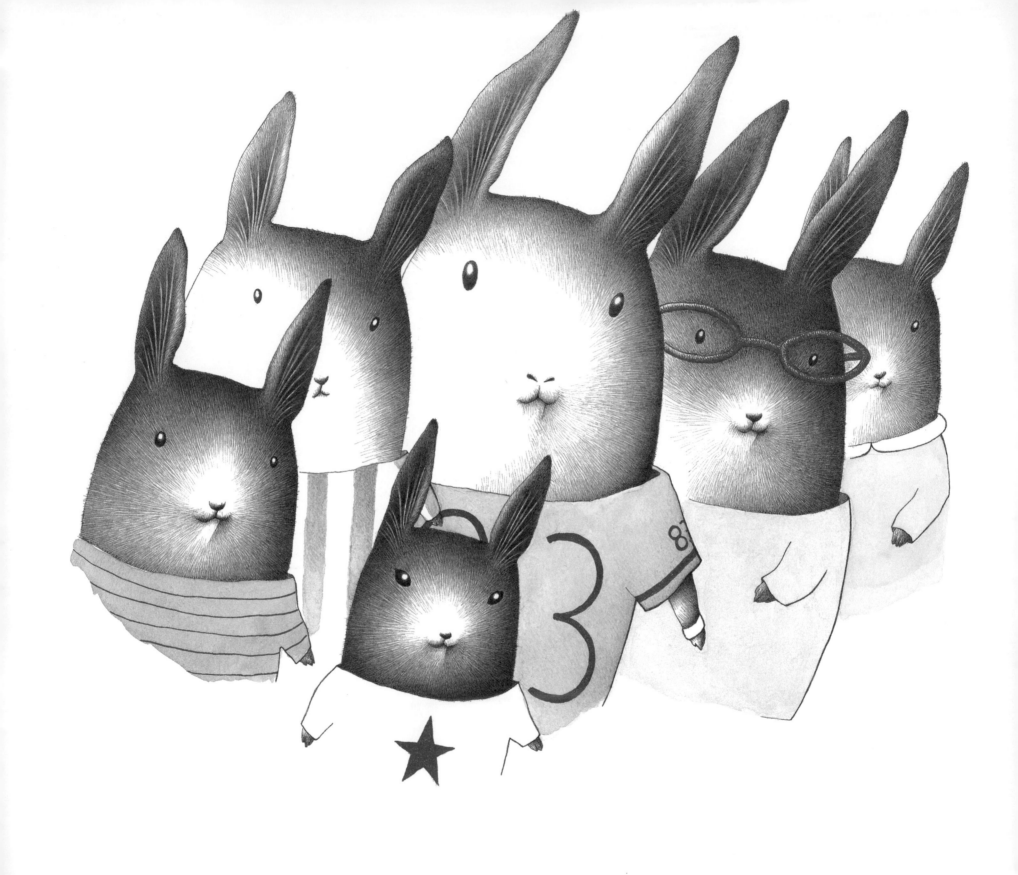

Pretty soon all the Bunnies wanted to play with the bubble wrap.

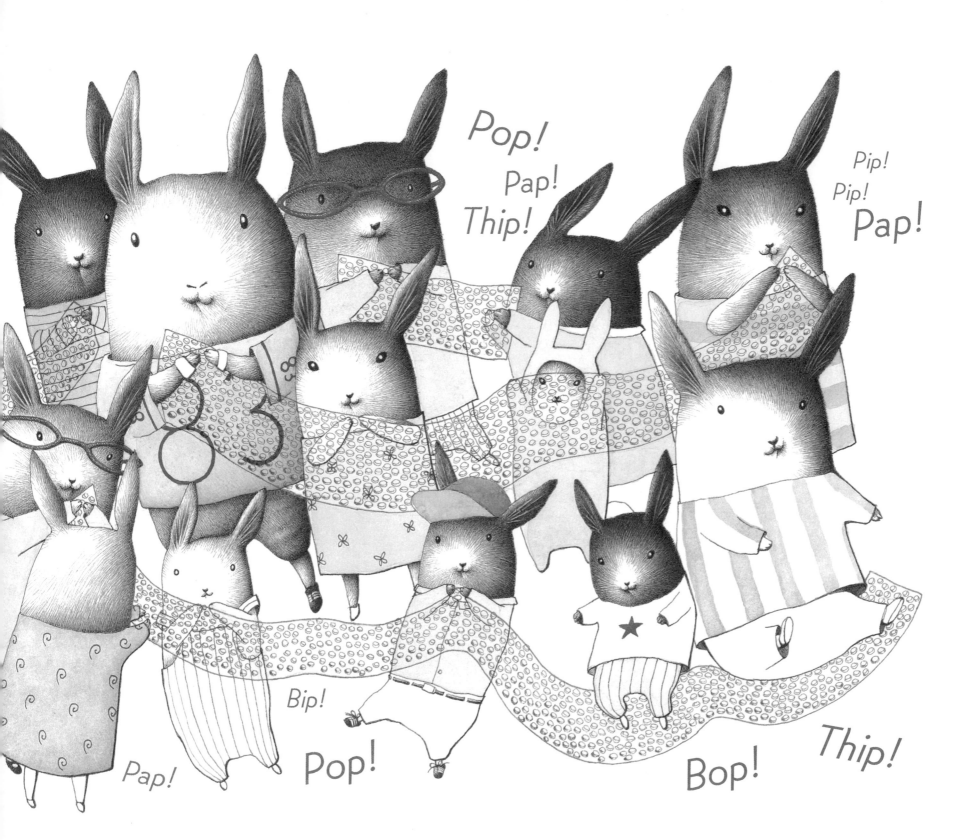

"Can you please be quiet?" Dad said. "We're trying to listen to the show."

"Here's a show for you, Daddy. GRRR, I am going to eat up the city!"

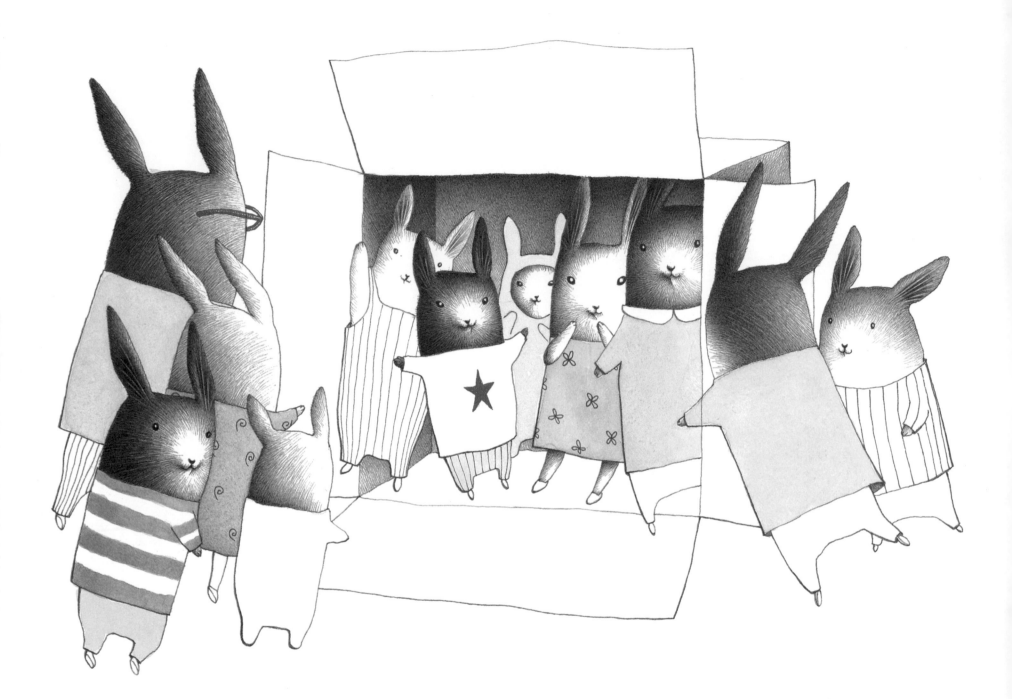

One by one, Chloe's brothers and sisters joined in.

Everyone wanted to be on television.

Everyone wanted to be with Chloe.

"That's enough!" Dad said. "Up to bed, kids."

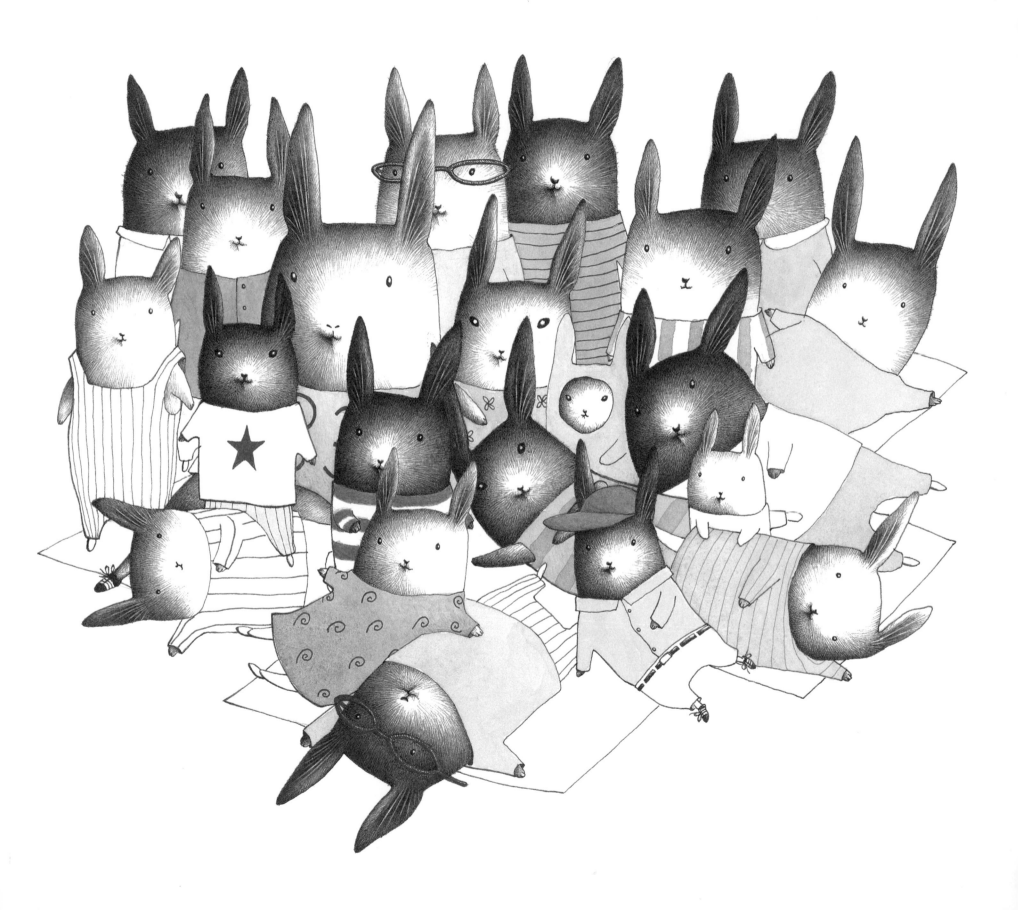

The Bunny boys and girls went up to their rooms.

"I wish we could pop bubbles and smash boxes every night," said Bobby.

"Good night, girls," said Mom. "Sleep tight."

Chloe fell asleep with her sisters snuggled all around her.

And even in her dreams, she could
hear the sound of popping bubbles.

Bip! Pap!
Pop!
Bop!